The Skipper's First War

A Skipper Series Novella

Mark Tissington

Wandering Tree Publications Limited

First edition 2022

ISBN Numbers:

Paperback, 978-1-7396384-5-0

eBook, 978-1-7396384-4-3

Dedication

To my family. They have no idea how awesome they really are!

Preface

This is the story of Reginald Gordon Hurton's experiences in World War One. He later achieved fame when he became known as 'The Skipper' but at this stage of his career he was a young deckhand apprenticed into a Hull trawler which became part of the Royal Navy Auxiliary Patrol, assigned to Patrol Area XI (Dover and The Downs).

In carrying out research and developing a plot for this story I came across the name of HMS Paragon. She was sunk while patrolling the anti-submarine barrage (which curved roughly between the south Goodwin Sands and the shallows WNW of Dunkerque). Online records seem confused and contradictory yet the Internet Archive holds The History of the Great War, Volume IV, Naval Operations (https://archive.org/details/navaloperations04corb/page/n7/mode/2up) which carries a detailed account of the action from official records.

Paragon was a destroyer which had the misfortune to encounter a German destroyer force on its way to penetrate the Dover Barrage and attack shipping. She was signalling her challenge when struck by a torpedo and massive gun-fire. She broke in two, sinking in around eight minutes. Her own depth charges detonated and killed many of the survivors, apparently. Another patrolling destroyer, HMS Llewellyn, was struck by a torpedo in the bow while attempting to rescue survivors but reached port with help, by steaming backwards! One section of the attacking force entered 'The Downs' anchorage west of Goodwin sands, sinking a merchant ship, firing on drifters and shelling Ramsgate and Broadstairs.

What I found most sad was the lack of certainty on the location of the wreck of HMS Paragon, where between 67 and 76 people perished with, reportedly, ten survivors. Given the Acasta class is listed with a complement of 73 people I do wonder if lists of the deceased crew are actually a full crew list (or she was lost with all hands - probably likely given that her depth charges exploded as she went down and Lewellyn was attacked while searching for survivors). By way of tribute I have listed below the names from the fullest list I could find from (https://www.coastalheritage .org.uk/Paragon.htm)

I note that one person on wrecksite.eu (https://www.w recksite.eu/userRequests.aspx?0?2?9537) posts a position very close to HMS Paragon's patrol area and which tallies with accounts from Calais of firing out to sea. Further-more, the description of the wreck fits reasonably well with contemporary accounts of the damage suffered by HMS Paragon but I am certainly no expert on wreck identifica-tion so please take this as my own opinion only. So far as I know however, no site is protected as an official war grave for those lost on HMS Paragon.

I therefore decided to mix fact and fiction, adding a survivor who figures in this story. In this way at least, I can pay tribute to those who lost their lives at around 10:50pm on 17th March 1917. I have also based my plotline for 20th April 1917 on the events descibed in The History of the Great War, Volume IV. Although no trawlers are mentioned in the narrative, I placed HMT Auriga close by.

I hope you enjoy this short tale. If you'd like to know more about my novel describing the adventures of a requisitioned trawler in the Second World War, writing, offers and the world of The Skipper, then please read my blog (https://mark-tissington-author.blogspot.com) and comment or send me your thoughts on the website using https://www.wtpublications.com/contact. Please let me know what you like, don't like, and even where you'd like to see the series go: I want to create a genuine community and hope you'll be part of it!

The Crew of HMS Paragon - sunk on 17th March 1917

ALLWORK, Henry W, Leading Signalman
ARCHER, Joseph, Leading Stoker
BALLS, Harry A, Signal Boy
BASHFORTH, James W, Able Seaman
BLAKEY, John W, Able Seaman
BOLINGBROKE, Russell, Sub Lieutenant
BOWYER, Richard G, Lieutenant (Captain)

BRIANT, Gordon W, Stoker Petty Officer
BROWN, Albert E, Leading Cook's Mate
BROWN, Alexander C, Stoker 1c
CASEY, Daniel, Able Seaman (CG)
CHAMBERS, Wilfred, Stoker
CLAY, James S, Able Seaman
COLTON, Terrence, Ordinary Seaman
COTTINGHAM, Victor, Able Seaman
CROWHURST, Edward J, Ordinary Seaman
DOUGLAS, Oscar R, Ordinary Seaman
DOWNER, William G, Stoker Petty Officer
ELKINS, George, Able Seaman (CG)
FARMER, Joe V L, Stoker 1c
FARRAR, Joseph, Chief Artificer Engineer
FEWTRELL, Sydney, Act/Engine Room Artificer
FINNERTY, Robert, Stoker 1c
GAMBLIN, Harry, Stoker Petty Officer
GIBBONS, Thomas, Ordinary Seaman
GOLD SMITH, Frederick K, Leading Seaman
GREASON, Herbert G, Act/Engine Room Artificer
GREAVES, Benjamin S, Able Seaman
GRIFFITHS, Leonard, Ordinary Seaman
HARFIELD, Frederick, Able Seaman
HARGREAVES, William, Stoker 1c
HAWKER, John, Leading Seaman
HEENEY, Thomas, Stoker Petty Officer
HOLLAND, Arthur, Ordinary Telegraphist
HOWELL, Joseph, Chief Engine Room Artificer 1c
JACKMAN, John, Gunner

JOHNSON, Jack, Stoker 1c
KENNETT, George W, Able Seaman
KNIGHT, Cyril A, Able Seaman
LAMB, Charles, Able Seaman
LAMBERT, John S, Stoker 1c
LANGRIDGE, Albert V, Chief Petty Officer
LANGTHORP, Thomas, Stoker 1c
LONG, Albert E, Leading Seaman
LOVERSEDGE, William, Able Seaman
MARSH, Edward A, Act/Leading Stoker
MAY, Sidney J, Able Seaman
MAYNARD, John, Officer's Steward
MURCHIE, Thomas C, Engine Room Art,
RNRNEEDLE, Frank, Stoker 1c
PACK, Walter, Stoker 1c
PADGETT, William F, Ordinary Seaman
PYLE, Thomas, Ordinary Seaman
RICH, Sydney, Able Seaman
RICHARDSON, Herbert F, Cook's Mate
SARGENT, James, Stoker Petty Officer
SCOTT, John R, Leading Stoker
SHADWELL, William C, Ordinary Seaman
SHARP, Stanley R, Act/Stoker Petty Officer
SHIRLEY, Henry, Able Seaman
SMITH, Robert, Stoker Petty Officer
SMITH, William H, Officer's Steward
STEELL, James, Act/Engine Room Art.
TAYLOR, Sydney C, Ordinary Seaman
TEW, Charles, Chief Stoker

TITFORD, William G, Stoker 1c
TROKE, William H, Ordinary Seaman
TUCKER, Albert E, Stoker 1c
TULETT, Charles H, Stoker Petty Officer
TURNS, William B, Leading Telegraphist
WALKER, Watson D, Stoker 1c
WALSHE, William H, Leading Signalman
WEBLEY, Herbert J, Lieutenant
WELLINGS, Thomas T, Able Seaman
WHITE, William G, Act/Leading Stoker
WICKERSON, Charles, Ldg Seaman (CG)
Note: CG is Coast Guard, Art. is Artificer.

Chapter 1

Baptism

AUGUST 1914

It had been a perfect night. The Moon was just past first quarter and the sky had been crystal clear. For a few days, the weather had been mild and the sea east of the Thames Estuary was glassy. So calm that the Moon and brighter stars were visible in reflection: waving, distorting, and dancing below their majestic celestial partners.

His Majesty's Trawler 'Auriga' was gathering together four merchant ships prior to escorting them into the English Channel. In the wheelhouse, the skipper, Bert Tinker, was in conversation with his first mate.

'Well Jack, let's hope we have a quiet night!'

'Don't worry Bert, if things get sticky, we've young Reggie to deal with the enemy eh?' He flashed a grin at their young apprentice who was taking a watch on the helm. Bert Tinker, their skipper, had known Sid, Reggie's father, for years and had been pleased to take Reggie on as an apprentice when asked by his friend. Sid had explained that his wife, Beatrice, didn't want both of her menfolk in one ship during a war.

The Moon westered, and the black sky greyed, making the world altogether less magical than it had seemed in the velvet darkness.

As their charges began moving, they pulled level with a freighter on their port side and settled to the routine. Jack was about to send Reggie for some tea when there came a boom that he could feel within his chest wall and a massive tower of water erupted above the freighter amidships. The freighter slewed off to port, mercifully away from Auriga, and began rolling over to starboard. She was slipping lower in the water as she slowed. The Tribal Class destroyer on the opposite side of the ship took off with a bone in her teeth, the white bow-wave visible in the slowly increasing light.

Bert ordered half ahead, swinging astern of the next freighter in line to search for survivors. Once through the line he went dead-slow ahead and had the lads out on the deck and in the bows to watch for survivors in the grey dawn.

They picked up six men from the water, one of whom died shortly after his rescue. As Reggie went to fetch tea half an hour later, one deckhand was swilling away what seemed like a vast amount of blood from the deck.

'Watch your footing young 'un. Poor blighter ripped the inside of his thigh on some torn plating and we couldn't stop the wound from bleeding.'

As Reggie turned onto the after-deck he gasped involuntarily when he saw a man with skin hanging in folds from a large part of his upper back. Their cook, Dougie Firsby, was giving him rum and went ahead of Reggie to fetch some bandages he had boiled.

'What happened to him Dougie?' said Reggie, hesitantly.

'Steam pipe to the assisted steering under their bridge ruptured as he was heading up to the deck, Reggie. Caught the poor sod square in the back. He can hardly breathe with the pain.'

Reggie had noticed the canvas shrouded form laid out over the stern grating as he had turned. He had always thought that death in battle would be glorious and instant, but was losing his boyhood innocence rapidly. War was turning out to be sordid and vicious.

As he reentered the wheelhouse with the tin mugs for Bert and Jack, he asked what had happened, Bert turned with a kindly smile, 'Most likely a submarine lad. Slippery they are, very tricky to find and even harder to kill.'

Jack nodded, 'I just wish we had a way to find the buggers Reggie. I'd give my eyeteeth to know where the damned things are!'

Reggie nodded, feeling numb.

Chapter 2

The Crew

FEBRUARY 1917

Reggie huddled into his duffel coat as he helped Lieutenant Mather test his hydrophone. This contraption comprised a beam suspended over the bulwark, from which hung a hinged steel rod with a bar at the bottom. At each end of the bar, an underwater microphone was fitted, designed to locate submarines from the noise of their machinery.

Mr Mather, as he insisted on being called, stopped and listened in his bakelite earphones, his eyes focused on infinity. The officer didn't seem to feel the cold, such was his level of concentration, but Reggie certainly did, and he flapped his arms around himself as he gazed out northward toward the Goodwin Sands. The sea was grey and white-capped and he could see surf charging at the exposed sands. He wondered whether the wheeling gulls felt cold as they flew squealing into the stiff breeze.

'That'll do Reggie, thank you. If you could lift the beam, we'll retrieve now.'

'Aye aye Mr Mather. Any success?' He reached for the line and began hauling up a little, before swinging the beam inboard once it cleared the bulwark.

'I think so Reggie, the propellor noises from the drifter, and especially the fast launch, were fairly clear. I used today to tune the equipment and I'll know more when we can test it while making way.' Mather came from a naval station near Aberdour and was on secondment to HMT Auriga, doing tests to refine underwater listening devices. In particular, he wanted to see if his redesigned hydrophone, lowered from a boom, could be used with the ship in motion. Ships on anti-submarine work had to stop in order to use their hull mounted hydrophones, but Mather's team were convinced that, by redesigning the microphone and separating it from the hull, they might detect submarines while moving.

As he finished stowing the gear, Jack Simmons, the mate, called over. 'Skipper says he's got some chart work for you to practice on Reggie, so cut along when you're done.' Jack was tough, but kindly. The trick to keeping him kindly was to follow instructions and work hard. Despite his love of labour, he was well respected by the crew because he could do any job onboard faster and better than anyone else.

Reggie checked the gear was secure and headed across the well-deck (the lowest part of the main deck) toward the access steps to the wheelhouse. Mr Mather's eyes followed the lad with a smile, he felt Reggie had a great future in front of him.

Inside, he went over to the small chart table in the rear starboard corner where the skipper, Bert was working over a chart.

'Ah, Reggie. How did you get on with the dark arts?'

Reggie smiled, 'Still can't get over how accurate Mr Mather can be Skipper. But he says it's not so effective when moving and worse in a seaway. It has to be better than nothing, though!'

'Aye, well Reggie, when men put their mind to a thing, they usually get it to work. When there's money to be made, they also tend to improve it quickly! Anyway, I've set you a couple of problems in your notebook if you'd like to get out the practice chart.'

An hour later, Bert had checked the lad's calculations and made one small suggestion to make life easier. They were running through lights and signals when Nobby, their wireless operator, popped his head out of his room, actually a small cubicle really.

'Signal from Dover, Skipper: Return to base with all speed'.

Bert's eyebrows lifted, 'Well now, I bet they're not calling us back to give us a week off! Reggie, nip down and call the new watch, would you?'

Reggie was already sliding down the ladder as Bert blew into the speaking tube. 'We're heading back to Dover, Henry, and they want us there yesterday, so I'll need our best speed.'

As dusk gathered, they anchored in Dover Harbour and Bert was rowed ashore. A signal lamp flashed and zigzag forks of lightning reflected in the rippled dark water below it. Jack kept the deck crew busy with gunnery drills, while the engineer had trimmers moving coal and helping with cleanup and maintenance. With drills done to his satisfaction, Bert called 'make and mend' until the Skipper got back, judging the lads would have a busy time ahead.

Bert reappeared at 20:00, muttering as he clambered over the bulwark. He clambered up the wheelhouse ladder and went inside. Jack sent a deckhand aft to get some tea for himself and the skipper. When they were alone, he raised his eyebrows, spotting that Bert was tapping his pencil on the chart table and biting his lip.

'Everything alright, skipper?'

Bert glanced up, 'Not sure yet Jack,' his brows knit together, 'a submarine, which has been attacking ships in the western approaches, seems to have got itself into the channel proper. Two merchantmen have been attacked today, one sunk and one damaged by gunfire. That ship survived because a light cruiser and two destroyers were leaving the channel at the right time, so the sub made itself scarce. Now, they want three ships with important cargoes escorting up to the Thames, so they're taking a destroyer from the Dover Patrol standby to escort the faster two and we get the slow one.'

Jack nodded, 'Well, there's potential for a nasty trip there Bert!'

Bert just nodded, frowning at his tide tables.

Reggie was having a mug of tea in the fo'c'sle, the cramped home for up to twelve men (currently four), right in the ship's bow. Wooden bunks, three high, were built into the sides and a tiny stove on the aft bulkhead gave heat. There were hooks on the bulkhead to hang wet gear but no drying room or wet-locker so, especially in heavy weather, the place had an air of steamy dampness. Their fish room had been converted to accommodation, with wooden bunks, hammock hooks, and a mess table, so eight men had moved from the forepeak to sleep, as had the gunners. Ratings all ate in there. The Skipper had his own cabin under the wheelhouse, while the mate, first and second engineers, and Mr Mather slept and ate in the aft cabin. The galley was in the deckhouse, forward of the aft cabin and engine room steps. Aft, there was a small shelter with a grating floor, to port of the depth charge chute on the afterdeck. This shelter functioned as their sea toilet with a better WC in the deckhouse. The deck house facility was popular because it was less dangerous in a following sea or during heavy rolling!

McNab, a slightly abrasive Scot who had a dim view of apprentices, poked his head down the fo'c'sle hatch. 'Mate wants ye aft wee 'un.' He withdrew his head and disappeared without waiting for acknowledgement. Reggie glanced over at his friend Colin Smith, the Lead Hand, who, in the early days, had been his mentor on deck when Jack was otherwise engaged. Colin gave a wry smile as Reggie pulled on his oilskin and boots, heading off to find Jack.

On the afterdeck, Reggie found Jack speaking to Mr Mather at the depth charge rack. The ship was equipped with two 120lb 'Type D*' charges, which resembled oil drums. They could be set to explode at forty or eighty feet when a barometric pistol fired. Mr Mather said they were more deterrent than threat because the 'proper' Type D contained a 300lb charge of explosive. According to Mr Mather, the Type D*, developed to prevent damage to slower patrol ships, could just about sink a submarine if dropped close enough to the hull.

Jack looked up as he approached, 'Now then Reggie, Mr Mather has asked for your help. We'll be escorting a merchantman up channel later today and you are more familiar with his gear than the others. The problem is, if we were to locate a submarine, you might be needed to go aft quickly to help drop a mine (both Jack and the Skipper still referred to depth charges by their original name of 'Dropping Mine'). Mr Mather says he only needs you to help locate the bugger, if we're using our mines, then his work is done. Think you can manage both jobs?'

Reggie nodded, smiling 'Yes Jack, no problem.'

The mate smiled at Mr Mather, 'Reckon I could run a battleship with two dozen like this one, sir!'

Mather looked at his watch, saying, 'I wouldn't bet against that, Mr Simmons!'

At 14:15 the next day, they made a rendezvous with the merchant ship, SS Rover, 8 nautical miles SSE of Swanage and turned to run on her starboard side, slightly ahead. Mr Mather had the gear over the side as soon as they were steady on their course. The sea was 'a bit lumpy' to use Jack's phrase, but he could hear underwater sounds, and by turning the underwater bar, he could estimate the direction of the sound source. Reggie had rigged the lines and blocks to enable a quick retrieval of the gear using the foremast boom. Jack inspected Reggie's work and turned to face them, 'It'll have to do I suppose.' He then stalked off aft.

Reggie beamed. Seeing Mr Mather looking quizzical, he said, 'The mate always says, if it's perfect, then it'll just have to do.' Mather shook his head, smiling.

Then began the tedium of routine escort work. Bert had once warned Reggie that patrolling would be 'a day of boredom followed by five minutes of horror' and their experiences had certainly shown that to be true. So often they would arrive to patrol the area where it was reported a submarine was operating, only to find a floating patch of flotsam and dead or dying men. If they were lucky, they would retrieve shivering survivors from the dark water, some with horrific injuries. Much of the time, it was just heaving water; empty save for Carley floats, broken wooden items. All sad reminders of souls taken from their families.

At 1830, the wind had veered westerly and the following seas were becoming heavier as dusk became night. They were south-southeast of Ventnor on the Isle of Wight, when Mr Mather stiffened.

'Reggie, I have a contact off the starboard bow. It's very faint'

Reggie sprinted to the speaking tube which had been installed on the outer wall of the skipper's cabin. Pulling off the cap, he blew hard.

A voice came from the tube, distorted but clear, 'Skipper here.'

'Skipper, Deck. Faint contact off starboard bow. Possible submarine. Mr Mather is monitoring'

Seconds later, they heard running feet as the six pounder deck gun was manned.

A few minutes passed, then Mather shouted, his voice tight with excitement, 'Definite contact, now fine on the starboard bow. I can hear it clearly above our own noise so it's close: they're probably getting into position for an attack on the freighter!'

Reggie relayed the message and heard the revolutions increase as the shout came down to prepare to attack. Mather wound up the hinged part of the hydrophone as he told Reggie to go aft.

Skidding to a stop on the wet deck near the chute, Reggie could see a charge already mounted in the 'retaining slot' of the ramp, the drogue (to slow its rate of sinking) loose at its side. Their ramp had been modified by their First Engineer, Henry Topping. He had welded an angle-iron frame to the top of the chute, which was wide enough to securely hold the fuel-drum shaped depth charge. They had rigged a safety strap made from a sling which looped over the top of the charge, holding it secure. To launch, they simply slipped the hitch securing the safety strap and let it drop, then they pulled up on two levers, one at each end, upon which were welded cam-shaped pieces of steel, high enough to dislodge the charge from its retaining slot and allow it to roll down the chute. Their second charge would then be loaded on to the retaining slot using a block and tackle. There was a shortage of the depth-charges so patrol ships were restricted to two each, which Mr Mather thought was laughable: a thought he kept to himself.

As the ship heeled to port, Reggie and Colin clung to the frame of the chute until the angle lessened. The speaking tube fitted to the side of the heads whistled. Colin answered and replied, 'Will do, skipper.' He turned, 'Looks like we're about to use a depth charge for real Reggie. Or a dropping mine, depending on whether Bert's listening!'

They had a dim, heavily shrouded red light shining down from the framework, just enough to see in pitch darkness, so Reggie readied himself and, when Colin nodded, he slipped the safety strap. Colin had remained at the speaking tube and suddenly started counting, 'Three, two, one, NOW!'

Reggie leaned on his lever as Colin stepped across to do the same at his side, the charge lifted and rolled away into the blackness. Colin, back at the speaking tube, said, 'Mine's away skipper.' They both ducked under the bulwark until they heard the crump and felt the thump, as their instructor had said. They then swiftly hoisted and loaded their last charge onto the chute as spray from the explosion spattered over them, carried on the following wind.

Shortly afterward they heard thudding feet approaching and Jack appeared in their dim circle of red light, 'Reggie, would you help Mr Mather, I'll lend Colin a hand here in case we need to drop another mine before you get back. Skipper wants a sweep with the hydrophone to see if the bugger has gone.'

Reggie made his way forward, grabbing the handrails welded to the deckhouse sides. The motion was very noticeable now, the westerly had stayed with them and the seas had become steeper as they reached shallower water.

After some wrestling, they got the beam over and dropped the hydrophone. The first quarter moon had broken through a gap in the scudding cloud and Reggie saw Mr Mather shaking his head, 'A lot of noise from the sea Reggie, sounds like shifting shingle, I don't think I'd hear a submarine now to be honest.'

After half an hour of intense concentration, Mr Mather sat up, 'This is hopeless Reggie. There's no way I could pick a submarine out of all this noise.'

As he spoke, they were suddenly illuminated in a glaring blue/white light. Reggie could hear voices yelling from above, then the light swung away. They could clearly see the beam of a searchlight pointing toward the shore. He registered Mather was frantically winding up the hinged section, and he prepared to pull the beam inboard.

Reggie's ears rang as the six pounder fired. He could smell cordite even with the wind off the deck. The searchlight remained trained toward the freighter and, waiting for the top of a wave, the gun-crew fired again. This time, white water was visible for an instant before the searchlight suddenly went off. Reggie turned toward where he assumed Mr Mather would be, his night vision having been destroyed by the searchlight, 'Ready to get the gear in Mr Mather?' He grabbed the beam to steady it as it came inboard and then made the gear secure.

'Reggie, I'm afraid the hydrophone will be of no further use until the seas moderate. Also, I want to check the cables before we need to use the gear again. I'll remove the units and their cables and check them below. Would you let the skipper know, please?'

Reggie gave the lashings a last check before heading for the wheelhouse ladder to update the skipper. When he had done so, Bert sent him to the galley for a brew. He was halfway down the mug of sweet tea when Colin entered.

'Look at you living the high life. Didn't Jack tell you to give me a hand?'

'I didn't see him, we were just securing the hydrophone for maintenance and the skipper sent me here for a brew. I'll come now.'

Colin shook his head, 'No need, it was just the safety strap was twisted but when the motion eased a bit, I did it. You finish your tea, I'll go find Jack, he may have gone below.' With that, he went into the corridor and down the engine-room ladder. A couple of minutes later, he reappeared, looking worried.

'He's not there Reggie. I'll go around the stern and then up to the skipper, would you check the fish-room and fo'c'sle please?'

Reggie downed his remaining tea and hurried forward, stopping to grasp on to a handhold twice. There was no sign of Jack in either location, so, bile rising in his throat, he doubled back, climbing the wheelhouse ladder to find the skipper looking pensive. Colin's face crumpled as Reggie shook his head.

Bert felt cold horror, 'You lads ask Mr Mather to co-ordinate a stem to stern search. Every locker, slush-well, everywhere. I'm going to send a signal. Alf, on the helm, looked sharply at the skipper, saying nothing.

Twenty minutes later, Mather and Colin reentered the wheelhouse. Jack was not found, and they faced the gut-wrenching truth that the mate was lost overboard. Bert's eyes welled up, and he dragged his forearm across his face.

Colin frowned, 'Why aren't we turning to search skipper?'

Bert took a deep breath, 'Because Nobby signalled man overboard, but my orders were to stay with the freighter. Their cargo is extremely important. I have no choice but to escort them to the Thames unless relieved by another escort.'

Colin's fists balled, and he drew breath to speak. Bert got in first, yelling, 'Don't make this harder that it already is Colin. Jack is my friend too!' They all winced as the wheelhouse door slammed and Colin disappeared down the ladder.

At the end of his watch, Reggie climbed into his bunk, essentially a partly enclosed shelf with a mattress and his kitbag for a pillow. He closed the curtain and stared at the bunk above for an hour before falling into fitful sleep. He dreamed he was in the water watching the ship steam away. The cold was eating into his core and he could hear Colin and Mr Mather shouting 'Jack!'

The rest of their trip was unhappy, but uneventful. They handed the freighter over in the Thames and set course for Dover. Bert ordered another wireless message to be sent to Dover, reminding them of a man overboard and giving the position. The signal was acknowledged, but when Bert reported ashore there had been no news of anyone picked up. They had to accept that Jack was yet another good man whose grave was the sea.

Bert and Colin had a long private discussion about difficult decisions a skipper has to make, which are necessary. Colin remained slightly distant, but after that long talk there was no longer a brick wall between them, so Bert was happy enough.

The day after their arrival, they had bunkered and taken on a replacement for the depth charge they had used. Bert reported in and was told that a new mate would be assigned to him as quickly as possible. He complained that his Lead Hand should be made mate, and he only needed a rating to bring him up to strength. His thinking did not influence the naval bureaucracy at all.

They went out on two routine patrols and helped muster ships to ensure they did not leave before the routine minesweeping was complete. After this they were given a rest day, re-provision and 'Make and Mend' in Dover harbour. They were supposed to get a four-day rest, but this seldom happened in their very busy patrol area. About two in the afternoon, a launch came alongside and a man came aboard, looking for the skipper.

Bert looked up as the new man came into the wheelhouse.

'Can I help you?'

The man scowled, 'Where's the skipper?'

Bert met his eyes and held them with a stony stare, 'Right in front of you. Perhaps you'd like to start this conversation again?'

The man didn't waver, 'Skipper. I'm Sid Cummings, your replacement mate.'

There was a pause, 'I'm Bert Tinker, the skipper of this vessel. I demand hard work, honesty, and fairness from my crew. Every one of them. You manage the lads but be warned, you have big boots to fill, and the wound is still raw; also these lads perform well, it's in nobody's interest to use a horsewhip if there's no need. Right, I'll show you to the aft cabin and introduce you to the crew.

During their tour of HMT Auriga, the new mate remained almost silent. He let out an occasional 'awright' in his south-east England drawl, but was generally uncommunicative. Bert missed the brief flash in the mate's eyes when he was introduced to Reggie, but Colin, who was also present, spotted it and wondered.

Bert tapped his teeth with his pencil as he watched Cummings head off for his meal that evening.

Chapter 3

The Mate

After their rest day, they were sent out to patrol the steel net barrage, laced with mines, which stretched for 28 miles, from the South Goodwin light, almost to Dunkerque. Its purpose was to prevent submarines, which menaced allied shipping, from entering the English Channel or laying new minefields. They accompanied four destroyers (Torpedo-Boat Destroyers as old hands in the Royal Navy called them) who would hold at given positions behind the barrage, while trawlers patrolled back and forth to reduce the threat of attack by a submarine and sometimes to detect them.

As they lay rolling slightly in an oily swell, Mr Mather was carrying out a listening watch, so far unproductive. Reggie had helped Colin grease the moving parts of the depth charge launching chute, then gone forward to see if Mr Mather needed anything.

As Reggie tidied up some cable, the mate came forward. The gun crew were closed up and the lookouts were on the upper bridge (a barrier with canvas screens was fitted on top of the wheelhouse to give a lookout position).

Cummings strolled toward their position, giving a treacly smile to Mr Mather.

'All's well here I trust, sir?'

Mr Mather pulled off his headphones, 'I'm carrying out a listening watch for submarines Mr Cummings, please allow me to get on with it.'

Cummings' smile got wider still, 'Sorry sir, I just wondered if I could steal young Hurton for a few minutes, please?

Mather frowned and pulled his headphones back over his head, saying, 'If you must, but I'll need him here in ten minutes.' He half closed his eyes as Cummings and his ingratiating smile oozed away aft with Reggie.

On the afterdeck, Cummings turned, pointing down to where a grease pot was upside down on the deck, its contents partially oozed out onto the planking.

'So, is this mess of your doing Hurton?' Reggie noted the words were a question, but the tone was an accusation. He knew he had put the grease back in the locker but he realised Colin might have got it out again afterward. Not wanting to involve his friend, he met Cummings' eyes.

'I don't think so Chief, but I may not have secured the locker door properly when I stowed it.'

Their eyes met briefly, then Cummings snarled, 'Now listen in, you arrogant little bastard. You're too much like your father for my liking. You are a member of this crew and you will ditch the Hurton attitude of being above everyone else and do it immediately. Do we understand each other?'

Reggie was slightly bemused, but his father had always said, 'Never wrestle a chimney sweep. It only gets you as dirty as he is.'

'Yes Chief, I understand. I'll clean up now if that's OK?' Reggie waited before doing so, not wanting to fall into any bear traps.

'Get on with it. And know that I'm watching you.'

Reggie replaced the drum in the locker, cleaned the deck with white spirit and scrubbed down, then sprinted back to Mr Mather.

Mather looked up as Reggie appeared, 'Everything alright Reggie?'

'Yes sir, I had spilled some grease and not noticed.'

Mather knew that Reggie always checked around before leaving any job, so he was surprised, but kept silence over such a trivial thing. He shook his head; they were all tired, maybe it was just his instinctive and instant dislike of the mate. He went back to his listening watch.

Two hours later, Bert blew down the engine room speaking tube, 'Full ahead please Henry, we're searching for a periscope.' One destroyer had signalled sighting a periscope, so they gave Mather a few minutes to search, but he heard nothing. He'd spoken to Reggie through the speaking tube and asked them to retrieve the hydrophone if required because they were going to do a high-speed search. Mr Mather was delighted. This was his opportunity to compare the sounds at speed in a calm sea. He knew he could compare his notes with the same activity in heavy weather and, subjective though some data might be, he could at least draw some provisional conclusions.

They steered a search pattern around the position of the sighting, leaving the destroyers and two other trawlers on station. Mr Mather said he had no contact and asked if the skipper could stop for a few minutes, which he reluctantly did. Once they were moving again Mather said that probably the sighting had been the fin of a harbour porpoise, which was the only sound he'd heard. After completing the search pattern, they rejoined their destroyers and reported no contact. Their patrol continued until one of the minesweeping trawlers who were working around a mile away signalled a definite periscope sighting. The destroyer had gone off on its patrol route so they steamed off at their top speed; the trawler signalled an approximate heading at the time of sighting. Mr Mather was listening hard as they approached the assumed position.

As they neared the likely position and slowed, Mather yelled he could hear the submarine off the starboard bow and heading across their course. Bert played it cool and continued on his course, then swung hard to port as they crossed the submarine's assumed track. He wanted the commander to think they'd missed him. They went full ahead until Bert deemed they had reached the position he would now be in. Mather had been slow getting the hydrophone in and Reggie raced aft to the depth charge ramp.

As Reggie emerged from behind the deck house Colin was listening to the speaking tube and pointing at the safety strap. Reggie went to remove it but found the knot was barred up so tight he couldn't get the strap off. Oddly, it was also wet, and he frowned as he pulled out his knife with its integral marlin spike. Glancing up, he caught Colin's eye, Colin nodded toward the strap and mouthed 'QUICK!' Reggie folded away the spike and opened the blade as he heard Colin speaking, 'Hang on Skipper, the safety strap is jammed!'

Reggie sawed and slashed away the strap and turned to stand by his lever as Colin, looking tense, said, 'We're ready Skipper, drop it now?' Reggie already knew the answer as the revolutions dropped off and they began to turn. As if on cue, the mate skidded around the corner.

'What the hell is going on? Are you two idiots able to drop a mine or not?'

Colin grimaced, 'We couldn't get the safety strap off Chief!'

'Hurton, go help Lieutenant Mather!' Cummings snarled.

As Reggie sprinted off to get the hydrophones ready, Cummings turned to Colin.

'Alright, so what happened?'

Colin shuffled, 'I was speaking to the skipper, Chief. He explained we were overhauling the sub, and he'd call when he reckoned we were over it. Reggie was still with Mr Mather, and I was just about to lean over to slip the safety strap as he arrived. He went straight for the strap, but I could see he was struggling to slip the knot. He cut it away, but the skipper said we'd gone over the sub by then.'

Cummings stopped and picked up the sling.

'Well, he would've struggled with this bloody knot!' He showed Colin a tightly jammed granny knot before going on, 'Right, do we have a spare strap?'

'In the locker Chief.'

'Fit it and tie it properly. I'm going forward to make sure Hurton hasn't buggered up the hydrophones! One last thing, whose job is it to secure the strap?'

Colin stared at the deck, 'Reggie usually does it Chief, while I rig for loading the next charge or secure the lever mechanism, but he wouldn't have tied a duff knot!'

'Maybe it was Father Christmas or a sea-sprite!' Cummings spat over the rail as he strode off.

On the foredeck, the hydrophones were in the water. Mr Mather was listening, eyes screwed shut. Reggie was at the speaking tube, ready to pass information to the wheelhouse. The mate arrived, his face a mask of anger. He stopped, but said nothing, waiting for Mather to finish. He had learned not to antagonise Mr Mather. During meals in the aft cabin, Cummings had learned that Mather was a civilian scientist who had been given naval reserve rank. Initially he saw this as good news but quickly realised that, while Cummings knew where the line lay with regular commissioned officers, this scientist was much less predictable and, therefore, harder to manipulate. So he waited.

After ten minutes, Mather pulled off his earphones, shaking his head. 'Nothing at all, I think they've dived deep and are sitting with neutral buoyancy or even on the seabed, just waiting us out.' Reggie informed the bridge and Bert asked them to maintain a listening watch, he would steam slowly in a wide search pattern to see if they could recapture the submarine.

Reggie looked up to see the mate beckoning him to the corner of the skipper's cabin. He saw some webbing hanging from Cummings' fist.

'Right you little sod, what the hell is this knot supposed to be?' Cummings snarled.

'I don't know Chief, it's nothing to do with me!' Reggie recognised the safety strap in Cummings' hand.

'Nothing to do with me! You lying little bastard, even your own mate says you tied it - and we lost the submarine as a result!'

Reggie paused, 'Chief, whatever Colin said, I would never tie a knot like that. Someone must have retied it.'

Mather looked up, 'Stand by the voice-pipe Reggie, please.'

Cummings turned, saying, 'You haven't heard the last of this Hurton!' before storming off.

Reggie felt numb. The knot had been wet and hauled tight, so whoever did that wanted it to be hard to unfasten. His logical mind was telling him there could be only one person who disliked him that much, but why risk losing a submarine like that? It made little sense, surely Cummings wouldn't stoop so low as to let their enemy escape!

Mr Mather looked quizzically at Reggie, 'What was all that about?'

'I'm not really sure, Mr Mather. The mate says I tied a bad knot, which resulted in the safety strap being jammed, so we missed a chance at the submarine. I've been securing gear since I was eleven years old. Even at that age, I wouldn't have tied a knot that bad!'

Mather shook his head slightly, caught between sympathy for the lad and naval discipline.

'Just keep on as you are Reggie. So far as I know you are respected for your work ethic, but also your seamanship. We all hit bumps and character clashes, but they pass. Keep going as you are, he'll get bored.'

Reggie flashed. A wry smile, 'Not much choice really Mr Mather. I'll be fine. So what's happening with our submarine?'

In the wheelhouse, Bert was getting frustrated.

'No Mr Cummings, I will not move young Hurton to a different job. This is his first mistake, if indeed he is responsible,' he raised his hand, 'I haven't time to argue. You're the mate; if the lad did wrong, then put him on a rubbish job for a day or two. With that one I'd try speaking with him, I've never had to go beyond that to steer him right!'

Cummings sneered, 'Well maybe that's his problem then skipper. If you don't mind me saying..'

'GET OUT CUMMINGS! I've said all I need to in this matter, now I have important things to deal with. Goodbye.'

The next four days were hell for Reggie. He swabbed out the heads at the end of every watch and Cummings intruded upon his meals and sleep as much as he thought he could get away with. On the fifth morning, Mr Mather sought Cummings out.

'It's time to stop now Mr Cummings. You had your fun, but I need Mr Hurton sharp. Are we clear?'

Cummings gave his usual sneer but his words were politeness itself.

'Of course Sir, I had intended to end his restrictions today, anyway.'

Mather was developing a genuine loathing for Cummings but tried to suppress it - on such small vessels a little negative attitude could have a huge effect on the crew. He knew Reggie was out on his feet however, and had felt bound to speak.

Two days after Mather's intervention, Reggie felt more like himself. Cummings had left him alone, and Bert also had a quiet word about riding it out: Bert felt sure Cummings would tire of goading Reggie - who dared to hope that Bert was right.

After his watch, Reggie went to the mess deck to eat before he slept. He nodded to the lads as he reached the bottom of the steps. He ladled himself some stew and grabbed a dumpling from the bowl. Dougie could work wonders with stewing beef! Reggie sat at an empty table where someone had left a newspaper open. It was a week old, but he hadn't read this one.

'Well, if it isn't Lord Muck himself.'

Reggie turned to see Fred Bilton, a deckhand and now a gunner, sneering at him. A swarthy man in his thirties, he'd always been quiet and, while they hadn't been close, neither had they traded insults before. He began to feel uneasy.

'Did I do something wrong, Fred? If so, I'm happy to apologise, but I'm just not sure what I did...'

Fred shook his head, 'Well lad, you came here and wormed your way in, then turned on your mates. Don't apologise though, you can't put that right with a quick sorry!'

'Turned on... Fred, I don't know what you mean!'

Fred clenched his fists, 'He doesn't know what I mean. Well, let's spell it out. You were born with a silver spoon. Daddy owns his own ship outright and is buying up others as we speak. You are guaranteed to be a skipper one day without lifting a finger. Oh, you've grafted, I saw that and thought you were alright; but now I know you've been badmouthing us to the skipper! You're beneath bloody contempt, so shut up and eat before I lose my temper!'

Reggie decided not to pursue it. He'd seen Cummings talking to the lads occasionally, it had often gone quiet as he approached but thought that was just the fabricated bad knot story. It seemed Cummings was still doing him down, but the subject was interesting. He ate up his food and left without speaking to Fred. He saw Stuart McNab and Graham Soper were sitting with Fred, and all three watched him as he left.

On deck, he let the cold air refresh him before going into the fo'c'sle. Colin was reading, so Reggie sat opposite.

'Colin, has the mate said anything about my father buying up ships?'

Colin looked bewildered, 'No Reggie. Not the mate, but Alf muttered something with your name in it yesterday. I couldn't hear what it was and wondered if I'd misheard. Has something else happened?'

Reggie frowned, 'Well, I think the mate is spinning yarns to the lads, which is trivial, but all his problems seem related to my father and the fact that he owns his own ship. Cummings is trying to turn that into a fleet of imaginary ships, probably to distance me from the lads, but it's a fiction! We lost my Uncle Charlie and because he was unmarried, an insurance payout came to my father who invested it back into the ship. It reduced the marine mortgage to a level he can afford, but he has no ambition to own more ships: he just wants control of his own!'

Colin studied his matchbox thoughtfully, 'I think you should write to your father and find out if he knows what Cummings is up to Reggie. At least you'll know what his motive is then.'

'You might be right there Colin, but to an extent the cause doesn't matter. It's the fact that Cummings is trying to get back at my father through me that's important. I'm thinking that the best way to deal with him is to get him to talk, to understand I'm not doing him harm, whatever beef is between him and my father.' Reggie said, thoughtfully.

Colin shook his head, 'Well, I doubt he will respond well if that's his motive. Just watch out that he doesn't twist whatever you say or do and use it against you Reggie. You're twice the man he is, and don't you forget that.'

After a smoke, they both turned in.

Reggie put the finishing touches to an eye-splice he had made for a halliard on the mizzen staysail, which was used to help keep the ship's head to wind if needed. Over the last few days, he had worked quickly and gone straight back to the mate to ask if he needed anything else doing when finished. The first time, Cummings had lifted an eyebrow before sending him to clean the mess room. As the mate got used to it the tasks became more varied. Reggie had thought there might be a tiny change in the tone of Cummings' voice and was encouraged. As he went on to the well-deck, Cummings spotted him first and called him over.

'Yes Chief, you wanted me?'

His eyes were like flint as he stared at Reggie, 'Frankly Hurton, I want you to jump over the side but I suspect you would disobey the order so I won't give it. No, I called you here to ask what you've been playing at for the last few days?'

Reggie frowned, 'I'm playing at nothing Chief. What I am doing is trying to prove that you're wrong about me. I'm not the person you seem to think I am, but words are cheap so I decided to show you.'

Reggie's level tone seemed to infuriate Cummings. For a moment he thought the mate would swing for him but Cummings stood, taking deep breaths and clearly trying to control himself. Cummings almost spat when he finally spoke.

'The same guff your father spouts Hurton. Holier than thou, soft-hearted garbage. You think you know your father, but you don't. Not at all. He found out that I sailed out of Hull when he interviewed me for deckhand. I could see his face change, all arrogant and superior like. The look he gave me wasn't fit for a dog, never mind a reputable seaman and his prejudice was obvious. Whatever he tells you, or lets you see, is not even a small part of him.'

Reggie was shocked at the outburst: he'd heard nobody in authority behaving so weakly. This was simply a petty grievance! He began to wonder if Cummings was actually mad. He had gone off at a right angle to the actual con-versation to begin another rant about his father. It seemed strange and not a little disquieting. In any event, a few of the lads in his father's crew were originally from Hull so that did for the prejudice idea!

As they stood to action stations later, for yet another fruitless submarine search, Reggie said, 'You were right Colin. Trying to win the mate over will never work. He's so set against my father that it's poisoned him. I think you might be right, I'll ask Father what Cummings' problem is, it might give me a way to approach him but I'm not so sure anything will!'

Colin nodded, 'Just take care Reggie. You and I both know that first mates can be a law unto themselves.'

Reggie looked over the stern, 'Yes I'm finding that out!'

With their patrol ended and a rest day given, Colin and Reggie went ashore, their first task being to post the letter. While he had time, Reggie also sent a telegram to Mother to tell her he was well, and a letter was on its way.

Colin had looked at him strangely so Reggie looked seri-ous and said, 'Colin, I want to be sure that Mother doesn't get straight on a train. Whatever he's done wrong, the mate deserves to be left with all his limbs intact!'

Colin slapped his back, chuckling, 'C'mon, let's find a coffeehouse, then a pub.'

Chapter 4

The Barrage

They had been out on the barrage, preventing freighters from sailing before their route had been swept. It was tedious work but Mr Mather kept Reggie busy with increasingly frequent adjustments and tests of his hydrophones. He confided he believed the redesign gave some improvement in what could be heard, but the performance tailed off at five knots. That, he said, represented a great improvement over the current hull mounted units and the data would allow them to further develop hydrophone design. He also believed improvements could be made in the hull-mounted units because of the work that had done.

'Reggie, when you hear of a submarine being sunk later this year, you can be satisfied you played a part in making detection better than before. Never forget that.' Reggie grinned back at him and Mather hoped the mate would lay off Reggie soon.

They had the forenoon watch that day so at 12:30 Reggie Sat with Colin in the mess deck for their lunch. Harry Jackson, a coal trimmer, and Alf Challener sat down at the same table. Reggie flashed a smile, asking 'How's things lads? All well I hope.'

Challener wiped his mouth with the back of his hand, 'Better than you are I suspect!'

Reggie's stomach sank, but he kept his face impassive and shook his head, 'Not sure what you mean Alf?'

'Well, we heard the sad news about your lass. Mavis is it?'

Reggies blood froze, 'What news?'

Challener leered, while Jackson shifted on his seat uncomfortably.

'The way we have it, she's engaged to be wed, and it'll need to be a quick wedding if you get my drift?'

Reggie gritted his teeth, 'I think you've been misinformed Alf.'

Challener gave a crooked grin, 'Well lad, you cling on to your hope but I live in the real world!'

Reggie shook his head, finished his last mouthful, and rose to put his plate in the rack. As he walked to the stairway Colin leaned toward his shipmate and hissed, 'You should be ashamed of yourself Challener.'

Reggie wasn't on deck so Colin went down the fo'c'sle ladder. Reggie sat with his head in his hands, shoulders shaking, smoke curling up from his cigarette. Colin was livid: the crew was disintegrating because of Cummings!

He was thinking of how to begin as Reggie fell back on the seat, in gales of laughter. Colin's mouth hung open.

'Oh Colin, I feel so much better now!' The laughter recommenced.

Colin smiled himself but shook his head, 'What's so funny about what they said?'

Reggie regained control, 'Because as I left the mess, a few things hit me all at once. First, this is Mavis: I've known her since we were both tiny and she categorically would not do what Alf suggested. Second, I had a letter from her two weeks ago and, if it were true, she would have told me. She can be infuriating and often ties me in knots but I know her and her family, she'd be straight. Last, why did it take so long for this to emerge? We've been at sea for days... No, this has got Cummings written all over it!'

Colin slumped in relief, 'I'm inclined to agree! Cummings has a lot to answer for. As lead hand I think I should go to the skipper Reggie.'

Reggie shook his head, 'I appreciate the thought Colin but that would give Cummings a platform to drop in more lies. Knowing Mavis as I do makes it certain that Cummings is behind it, but Bert would need proof before he could act. I think that respectful but firm denial is needed and I think I'll change my tack with the mate.'

Colin shrugged, 'Well, if that's what you prefer, but I hope you know what you're doing!'

That evening, Bert briefed the crew: they were to proceed to the Dunkerque end of the barrier in company with a minesweeping trawler. Once there, they would re-provision and bunker if necessary, before relieving the ships currently on post. They would be performing the same duties as they had at the other end of the barrage, shepherding and stopping freighters entering an unswept area.

They were to gather and accompany two ships who were southbound on the following morning and be back on station by midnight of the following day to begin their task.

All went to plan until they reached the Avant Port in Dunkerque. They clearly weren't expected and Bert tied up on the Quai Du Risban. He yelled down to the well, 'Reggie, would you nip ashore and see if you can find out what's happening please?' Reggie waved and went below for his notebook. Cummings entered the wheelhouse shortly afterward.

'Skipper, does it have to be Hurton to go ashore? There must be better p...'

Bert interrupted, 'Mr Cummings, do you speak French?'

'No sir, I don't. But I'm sure I can make a bunch of frogs listen to me.'

'No, you won't Cummings. Hurton knows this port and speaks passable French. He goes. Carry on.'

Cummings fumed his way down the wheelhouse ladder. As he strode across the well deck he heard a voice call.

'Ah bonjour Monsieur Reggie!'

'Bonjour Monsieur Decalf. Comment vas-tu aujourd,hui?'

'Je vais bien, merci!'

Glaring at the quayside, he was greeted with the sight of Hurton's hand being pumped by an overweight man in a dark blue jacket and peaked cap. He turned away in disgust.

Thirty minutes later they were moored and receiving coal, fresh water and supplies of food. When the minesweeper had also bunkered and replenished supplies, they steamed away from the Quai with M. Decal waving them off.

As the rippling water of the Chenal gave way to open water, the ship gently rolled to a cross-sea and arrived on station at buoy 23a, around 10 nautical miles ENE of Dunkerque, just before 19:00 on Saturday March 17th 1917.

At 22:45 Reggie was on his way to fetch a brew for the wheelhouse when he bumped into the mate. On hearing Reggie's voice, Cummings told him to wait. He came close to Reggies ear.

'So you think your girl is lily white I hear.'

Reggie smiled in the darkness, 'Not at all Chief. I know for a fact that she is. I'm afraid you were misinformed.'

Cummings' breath, hot and reeking of stale tobacco disgusted Reggie as the mate replied, 'So you're accusing me of lying are you Hurton?'

'No Chief, definitely not. I discounted the idea that a ship's officer would concoct such a story so I naturally assume it's the person who told you who made an error. Perhaps there's another girl in Scarborough with the same name. That would explain it.'

Cummings was fizzing, 'So how come you're so sure then? Psychic?'

Reggie replied cheerfully, 'No Chief, I don't believe in that kind of thing. I can't reveal how I know, it's deeply personal, but I definitely know, one-hundred percent, that she did not do what I was told she had.' He waited for the explosion but none came. He could practically hear the gears of Cummings' brain grinding as he searched for a way to say more without revealing that he was the author of the tale, but none came.

With a voice coated in acid, Cummings said, 'Touching faith you have Hurton, let's hope it's not misplaced. Now get out of my sight.'

'Will do Chief. Thanks.' He left quickly before Cummings could react to the sarcasm.

Reggie joined the lookouts in their brew, listening to them arguing about flashes they had seen to the northwest. He was taking back empties at 23:25 when he heard Nobby Williams, the wireless operator, saying to Bert that a submarine had torpedoed two destroyers off buoy 11a, around 12 miles northwest of their position. Bert called out to get the word to the crew. He had a feeling they'd be in action soon. Spotting Reggie, he asked him to run to the aft cabin and warn Mr Mather.

Reggie knocked on the door and entered when he heard a voice. Cummings sat at the cabin table smoking and Mr

Mather was reading with his cabin door open (it was called a cabin but resembled a cupboard). Cummings spat out a strand of tobacco.

'What the hell are you doing in here Hurton? Sod off!'

Mather called angrily, 'Belay that Mr Cummings! Why are you here Mr Hurton?'

Reggie described what he had heard and relayed the skipper's message.

Mather smiled as he left his cabin, 'Thank you Reggie. I did an adjustment to the hydrophone, I think we'd better re-rig it sharpish!'

Reggie grinned 'Aye aye sir!'

Cummings was left staring at the bulkhead as they left.

Reggie and Mr Mather assembled the gear using a dim red light under the turtle-back. Once Mather had checked the gland seals, they attached the gear to the beam and hooked it onto the lifting gear. Reggie checked the safety latch on the hook was correctly set, and they were ready!

At 23:40 the monitor anchored inshore of them signalled. They were to set a course for the last location of HMS Paragon, one of their own destroyers, and begin a listening watch as well as searching for further survivors. They were given the position and told to make best speed. The minesweeper was also tasked with attending.

When they arrived at the position, they stopped and lowered the hydrophones. For five minutes, Mr Mather listened but could only hear air escaping from the wrecked destroyer.

A sharp whistle came from the speaking tube next to him and Reggie jumped. He took off the cap, 'Deck here.'

'Reggie, it's the skipper. Could you ask Mr Mather if he can spare you for half an hour, please? I'd like to get our youngest eyes on the turtleback and around the stern to assist the lookouts.'

'Will do skipper, if you don't hear otherwise I'll be on the turtleback.'

'Good lad Reggie.'

Mr Mather said he'd shout up if he needed help so Reggie climbed up the access ladder, which was tricky with the gun platform restricting room. Charlie Phillips and Fred Bilton climbed up just behind him.

A couple of minutes later two searchlights lanced out from the wheelhouse wings and began slowly playing on the sea's surface. The ship edged forward at about three knots, every eye alert for signs of life.

In the wheelhouse Cummings was with Bert when Nobby popped his head in, 'Another wireless message gents. Lafore is escorting Llewellyn, which was the second ship attacked. A torpedo blew off her bow, it seems. She's steaming backwards toward Dover to keep the pressure off her front bulkhead! Anyway, Lafore has corrected her earlier message. It wasn't a submarine which launched torpedoes, it was a group of enemy destroyers!'

Cummings' voice came from behind Bert, 'And we're directly on their return course, lit up like Christmas!'

Bert frowned, 'I don't think that follows Mr Cummings. Given they sank a ship and damaged another in this location, I would say they're unlikely to return this way. In fact, as they've penetrated the barrage to do this, I'd be surprised if they didn't call it a good nights work and return through the barrage immediately afterward! We will follow our orders and continue to search.'

The minesweeper signalled using an Aldis lamp: they were sweeping back toward the barrage in case the enemy had laid mines.

Cummings was doing the rounds of the lookouts and Reggie heard his grumbling and swearing as he climbed up to the turtleback. He was muttering to Bilton who suddenly exclaimed, 'Destroyers? This is bloody madness!'

As Reggie shook his head at such negativity, the slowly sweeping beam caught a shape in the water and snapped back. It was a Carley float but, sadly, empty. The beam waved about slowly and there was more detritus in the water. Reggie assumed that the tidal flow was bringing remains of the sinking back toward them.

They crept forward, the searchlights gently waving left and right so the debris field was well covered. After ten minutes, the flotsam began to thin out. Cummings had gone, which was a boon so far as Reggie was concerned. Mr Mather called up, 'Skipper says another five or ten minutes gentlemen, then we'll turn back and cover another strip. I'll continue listening on my hydrophones.'

The water looked clear ahead, and the searchlights had resumed slow sweeping. The minutes ticked away and Bilton was cursing under his breath, muttering about wasting time and fighting destroyers. Reggie froze, yelling, 'Sweep back with the starboard searchlight please. I saw something!' At the same moment, Mr Mather called again.

'I can hear something too. It's faint and I'm not sure what it is but it's new to me!' He dashed over to the voice-pipe.

Cummings and McNab were on the starboard side of the well-deck. Cummings suddenly pointed, shouting, 'Sir, Mr Mather! There's a floating mine in the water off to starboard!' Mather informed the skipper who called all stop and the ship coasted to a halt. Reggie had called for the searchlight to go to starboard a little and called again, 'There. It was there again! I'm almost certain there's a man in the water!' Phillips turned and nodded agreement, calling to Mr Mather that he could see it too.

Cummings and Mather both set off to speak with the skipper.

In the wheelhouse, Bert took off his hat and scratched his head. Mr Mather and Cummings both looked at him anxiously.

'It's a terrible decision to make gents, but I can't risk the ship if there's a minefield ahead. We're stemming the tide, or we were, so that damn thing must've come from ahead of us. To go searching for a sighting which might save one man, set against the danger to everyone on board, it doesn't look right to me.'

Cummings piped up, 'I agree sir, and there's also the possibility, however remote, that destroyers could be about!'

Bert looked at him sharply.

Mr Mather grimaced, 'Two men saw something in the water skipper, and I also heard a strange noise in my hydrophones. I do respect your thinking about the relative danger but, well, we were sent to pick up any survivors and he can't last much longer.'

Bert nodded, 'That's what's preying on my mind Mr Mather. If it is a man in the water...' He thought, 'Mr Cummings, would you call down and ask young Reggie to come up here, please?'

Cummings turned, rolling his eyes as he did so, which did not go unnoticed.

'Hurton, to the wheelhouse and look sharp!'

'Will do Chief,' said a voice from the darkness.

When Reggie arrived Bert put his hand on his shoulder, 'How certain are you Reggie? That what you saw was a man in the water I mean.'

Reggie nodded, 'I'd say seventy-five percent skipper.'

Bert shook his head, 'I'm not sure that's enough lad.'

Reggie's jaw set, 'If it's the floating mine that's a problem skipper, I'd like to take a boat if we can keep a searchlight shining in that direction? We'd be unlikely to trigger it if another came adrift and with a shallow draft we'd not set off moored mines.'

Mr Mather nodded, 'I'm also happy to go skipper: in a boat we're reducing the danger to the crew and to this ship. Nothing to lose I'd say.'

'Count me in skipper, if I can be relieved for a while,' came Colin's voice from behind the wheel.

Dougy Firsby was delivering a brew for the skipper, 'Me too skipper, it'll get me out of the galley.'

Bert let a belly laugh out, 'Comes to something when a skipper gets browbeaten by his own crew!' Go on then the lot of you. You'd better bring me a survivor mind!

Cummings stepped forward, 'I'll get the boat in the water skipper and get someone to take over the wheel.'

Ten minutes later they were in the boat, having been joined by Stuart McNab, which surprised Reggie. Mather took the tiller and the four crew pulled an oar each.

Reggie, sat next to McNab piped up, 'Thanks for coming along Stuart.'

McNab seemed uncharacteristically subdued, 'Aye, well, I've my reasons young 'un.'

Mather wanted to lighten the atmosphere, 'Sounds ominous Mr McNab, care to share?'

McNab was silent for a few seconds then spoke, 'Permission to speak freely, sir?'

'Always Mr McNab, always.'

'It's just, well, I could'nae see any bloody mine!'

There was a long silence before Mather spoke again.

'Thank you for your honesty Mr McNab. I'd like you all to keep that between us, please? At least for the present.'

The four men murmured assent as Mather slapped the gunwale, 'Right, let's find the skipper his survivor shall we?' They were nearing the area where the searchlight played on the sea.

They started rowing an expanding box but after five minutes had found nothing except a waterlogged tea-chest. Mather abruptly called 'Oars,' to stop them pulling, and listened. They all heard the noise: it sounded like singing!

Mather became businesslike, 'Give way together lads, nice and steady.' They all strained to hear as they pulled. The noise was intermittent but definitely getting louder.

McNab suddenly laughed, 'My God! It's Eternal Father!' the sound paused again but then they all heard it, the seaman's hymn, '...for those in peril on the sea.'

Mather told Reggie and McNab to ship their oars and use hand lamps to search for the survivor. Mather bellowed, 'Keep singing man, we can't see you!'

The weak and thready voice began again, this time interspersed with sobs.

Reggie spotted him first and pointed. As Mather turned slightly, Reggie hung over the gunwale, arm outstretched. The man was clinging to what looked like part of a Carley float. As they came close, Mather called 'Toss oars!' and the two rowers lifted their oars vertically up. McNab shone his light over Reggie's shoulder as the man raised an arm and Reggie grabbed it.

'I've got you,' said Reggie as the man gazed up at him without response, 'Mr Mather, would you get his other arm so we can pull him in?'

They eased the man toward the stern and McNab reached over to gather his feet. Curiously, the man wore a single shoe, which thumped on the hull as they rolled him in. Reggie patted his shoulder, 'You'll be alright now, friend.'

Mr Mather grabbed the blanket and towel somebody had thrown into the boat. He told Reggie to towel the man vigorously on face, arms and legs to restore circulation, then wrap him in the blanket. He also had a hip flask of rum and water which Bert had handed to him from a locker in the wheelhouse but decided to wait until they had assessed the man's condition.

They pulled hard back to the ship. Bert had doused the searchlights but a red guiding light was showing from the upper bridge.

Once back on board, the rescued man began to revive. Mr Mather gave him a small amount of the dilute rum and Dougy slipped off to fetch some broth. He gave his name as sub-lieutenant Fortescue-Smythe and Mather had him taken to the aft cabin. He asked Mather to write the names of the men who had rescued him and especially the lad who reached down to him in the water. Mather explained Reggie's pivotal role in the search and the young officer shook his head slowly.

'Well, young Hurton is certainly no 'ordinary' seaman Lieutenant Mather.'

'Indeed not. His father runs a trawler out of Scarborough and young Reggie did a trip to Iceland, albeit during the summer holidays, at the age of ten!

As Mather stood, Fortesque-Smythe asked if he could borrow something to write with, so Mather fetched a pencil from the drawer in the cabin table.

When Reggie came down with dry clothes and bedding, the young officer was asleep, so Reggie added an extra blanket and left. That was almost the last he saw of Fortesque-Smythe, though he always felt glad that he'd helped save a man in those circumstances.

Reggie went below at 02:30, knowing he had to be ready for the morning watch at 04:00.

When his alarm sounded, he swung his feet to the deck. He knew it would be fatal if he didn't get moving when he was so short of sleep.

In the wheelhouse, Cummings was on watch. As Reggie came in his mouth twisted.

'Well, well. The hero of the hour himself.'

Reggie shook his head, 'No Chief, I was on lookout, then just part of a boat crew. All I did was my job.'

'More false modesty eh Hurton? You never stop dancing to Daddy's tune do you?.'

Reggie ignored the ridiculous behaviour.

'Would you like a brew Chief? Or is there something else you'd like me to do?

'Relieve Phillips on the flying bridge. You're on lookout seeing as you're so good at it!'

'Aye, aye Chief!' Reggie said with a smile. He was glad he'd put his duffel on and waved to Colin who was on his way in to relieve Cummings.

Up on the top bridge it was chilly, but not winter chilly, he told himself. Phillips told him they were heading back to drop their rescued man onboard the monitor before resuming their original position for marshalling merchantmen. The lookout job gave him chance to think, and he realised that simply ignoring Cummings or politely refuting his wilder lies was actually working. Cummings tended to stop after such a reply, he'd noticed.

They came alongside the monitor and their man was hauled aboard. As they fended off, he looked up and spotted Reggie; he gave a grateful smile and a wave, to which Reggie responded in kind.

After a few days of routine ship marshalling, they were heading to Dover for a rest day. As they stowed away the hydrophone gear Mr Mather was worrying. He had noticed Reggie's responses to Cummings' attacks and knew why Reggie was doing it, but he hoped Cummings didn't escalate things.

Chapter 5

The Message

Reggie sat in the fo'c'sle reading his father's letter yet again. Father did indeed know Cummings: he had interviewed him and thought him promising. He then made some enquiries among contacts in Hull and it emerged that Cummings had been a lead hand for three years, not an experienced mate as he had claimed. He had met with him to tell him he was unsuccessful and had received a lot of threats. Of course Father had faced him down, but it was when Cummings realised how many contacts Father had with good men in Hull that he stopped. Shortly afterward he had either gone up to Fife or to the west coast, Father couldn't recall. He closed by telling Reggie to stick to his principles and things would eventually be resolved.

Reggie couldn't see that this information was particularly helpful, he would have guessed at something similar. After some thought, he decided he would just have to sit it out. There *was* McNab's conviction that the mine didn't exist, but of course whether something could or could not be seen on a dark night, especially when only two people were present, was not clear evidence that misconduct had taken place.

And so he ground it out for the next few days. Cummings was riding him and even had a stab at Colin occasionally, but they both carried on doing what they did with as much confidence as they could muster and a cheery smile.

All went well during their remaining time on patrol until they turned away from the muster point at the Goodwins end of the barrage, heading for Dover. Reggie had done a navigation exercise with Bert and Cummings clearly believed that Reggie was using his time with the skipper to brief against him. This manifested in a string of extra jobs and muttered insults. Reggie suddenly realised that Cummings wouldn't know that Bert and his father were friends. Perhaps that was why Bert's apparent familiarity with Reggie grated on him so much!

It was after their next rest day before the opportunity arose: Reggie manned the wheel while Cummings was on watch. Reggie waited until he had done some chart work and written up the log before speaking, 'Chief, can I just mention something please?'

Cummings looked over, 'Please, do let me have the benefit of your great experience Hurton!'

'Well, forgive me, but it always seems like it makes you angry when the skipper has me in here to do chart work,' he noted Cummings' darkening face but pressed on, 'but I just wanted you to know that this isn't favouritism, it's that the skipper has been my father's friend for years.'

There was a long silence. Cummings' hands shook and his face looked pale and mottled. He closed his eyes for a second before speaking.

'You clever little git! You think that setting the skipper up as Uncle Bert will do you any good? Maybe you think it'll scare me knowing you're all in the same, cosy club? Well, you're wrong, dead wrong. In fact, I think this attempt to belittle me reveals what a sneaky little shit you really are! I tell you what I'll do. I'll leave you alone if you're that scared. I won't try to improve your performance - but I will certainly make sure your pal Colin takes the load! Oh, and if one word of this conversation gets out to anyone, I swear by everything I hold dear that I will kill you!'

His voice had risen to a shriek, and he trembled with rage. Reggie looked at the deck, thinking hard.

'Sorry Chief, I didn't mean to rile you.'

Cummings grinned savagely, 'Much better attitude Hurton. More of that, please! Now shut up.'

Reggie couldn't imagine the depths of character weakness and self-doubt evidenced by Cummings' outburst. Perhaps he had been naive to think Cummings would understand, but the twisted belief about his motivation and the crazed reaction, well, it was out of all proportion.

Reggie stayed on the wheel until the end of the first dog watch, when he went to eat. Colin had been helping the engineer with some repairs and Reggie kept quiet until they were back in the fo'c'sle. He briefly outlined the conversation, then waited in silence until Colin had digested it.

'The man is truly unhinged Reggie. We have to go to the skipper with this.'

Reggie stroked his chin, 'I think you're right, but put yourself in Bert's shoes. It would be difficult for him to criticise his first mate based on our word. Look, I know he's aware of Cummings' attitude because he told me to work my way past it. There's plenty of evidence that I've been working hard to do just that, so I think he'll realise soon that Cummings is a problem.'

Colin sighed, his shoulders slumping, 'Reggie, you always take the load yourself. We're a crew, we work together, at least we did until Cummings came onboard. You don't have to suffer instead of us.'

He looked at Reggie and saw the set of his jaw.

'Alright, I will hold off for the time being, but Reggie, in my role as lead hand I reserve the right to take this to Bert when I deem it's necessary. Agreed?'

Reggie met his eyes, 'Agreed, and I trust you to do that only when things get dire. But to be honest, if he keeps his word, he'll be after you now, not me.'

Colin shook his head, 'Yes, you said that. Thank you... Ex-mate! Oh, and pass me a mint imperial, since you've thrown me to the wolf!'

Chapter 6

The Charge

R eggie sped up to the wheelhouse, wondering what the skipper wanted. As he entered, there stood Cummings looking very concerned at Bert's side.

'Did you want me skipper?'

'I did Reggie. Mr Cummings has something to say which I'd like you to hear.'

He turned to Cummings with a nod.

'Well young Hurton, I've had some distressing news which I feel we need to discuss openly.'

Reggie grinned, 'No problem Chief. Whatever you need.'

'Well, you may smile Hurton but I for one don't believe this is funny. I know and have witnesses, that you have been peddling false information, a pack of lies to be blunt, to members of the crew. Some suggest to me that your aim is to set up a faction in the crew which does not accept my authority and that is tantamount to inciting mutiny!'

Bert watched carefully as Reggie gasped, his mouth open. He was shaking his head and about to speak when Cummings held up a finger.

'None of your wriggling young man. I have people who will testify to your actions. I have spoken with the skipper who tells me he knows your father. This gives me a chance to avoid Royal Navy discipline which I judge to be too harsh in your case. The skipper will speak with your father, and we will inform him of your actions. We then hope that we can come up with a plan to guide your path. Son, you are an excellent seaman for your age but have a habit of overestimating your experience and your place in the crew. With your father's help and cooperation we believe we can turn you around. Have you anything to say?'

Reggie took two slow, deep breaths, 'I do Chief. I'd like to ask which combination of McNab, Bilton, Soper and Challener will be testifying, as you put it?'

Bert recoiled, 'Reggie, that's enough! Get back to your duties before I rethink the way we handle this!'

Reggie nodded, 'Sorry skipper. Will do.' He walked out of the wheelhouse with his head down.

Colin shook his head when Reggie finished telling him. He realised what hurt Reggie was that Bert believed Cummings.

'Reggie, you and I know what your father knows. Cummings didn't make the grade, and our experience shows your father's opinion was spot on. You or I might have learned from that and improved, but Cummings simply twisted it in his head until he became the victim. He couldn't accept what is obvious to the rest of us, he simply isn't good enough. He might even be a coward if McNab is right about the imaginary mine. No, I think you should stick it out a bit longer. If Cummings is going to slip up, it'll be when he thinks he's on top. Just do your job and make sure I see everything you do when we're at the depth charge rack - then I can testify for your work.'

Reggie nodded glumly as he drew on his smoke, spitting out a stray strand of tobacco as he pulled out the cigarette and exhaled.

Chapter 7

The Battle

I t was 20th April 1917. The weather was noticeably milder and things had settled down on board. Reggie had been subdued and Cummings was strutting like a cockerel when his admirers were around him. McNab had disappointed Colin and Reggie by seemingly rejoining Cummings' camp. Reggie wondered whether Mr Mather had ever told the skipper about McNab's mine story but he had put it out of his mind. Taking Colin's advice and his father's teaching, he did his work and stopped fretting about things he couldn't control.

They were on a night patrol off the Goodwins and it was clear from around 23:30 that enemy destroyers were again breaching the barrage. They had shelled Dover, and Commander Peck on HMS Swift, a British destroyer, signalled Auriga to take up position between buoy 3a and the Goodwin Sands. He warned them that an enemy force was loose, and the reserves had sailed from Dover.

Bert had them at action stations with the deck gun loaded. Given that they could be attacked by a destroyer or destroyers, he put his youngest eyes on the flying bridge and sent the mate to the gun platform to oversee operations. Mr Mather was told to stow as much of his equipment as possible.

At 00:45 there was a lot of gunfire to the west and shortly afterward a massive fire started, clearly a ship was ablaze. At 01:00 they heard a powerful ship approaching and simultaneously HMS Swift came tearing past firing away from them. Reggie saw a flash beyond Swift and a shell burst in the water off their beam. Soper, also on lookout, screamed and fell backward. Reggie shone his red flashlight and saw that shrapnel had laid open Soper's scalp to the bone but luckily it had been a glancing blow. He yelled he would fetch a first-aid kit from the wheelhouse and took off like a rabbit. He breathlessly asked the skipper if he could take a kit and had already grabbed and turned before Bert said yes. Mather passed Reggie as he tore off upwards and entered the wheelhouse.

'Anything I can do to help?' He sounded breathless. Bert glanced round.

'Yes, can you go to the gun platform and make sure they know there is a British ship between us and the enemy?' They all ducked as a shell screamed overhead, 'Oh and they're firing at Swift, not us, so please tell the lads to stand firm. The mate is there with them.'

Mather dashed off and arrived at the gun platform as the exchange of fire seemed to die off. He passed on the message and asked where the mate had gone to.

'Haven't seen him Sir, I assume he's in the wheelhouse,' said Challener as he slewed the gun hopefully.

'Alright, I'll find him there, thanks.' Mather left and climbed the steps to the wheelhouse. As he went in Cummings came up behind him, panting.

Cummings gasped. 'Did you call for me skipper?'

Bert turned, 'No? Why do you ask?'

'One of the lads at the gun said you'd called, must've misheard. I'll get back there.' He ran out of the door.

Mather's brow creased, 'Skipper, a word when you can spare a moment, please?'

Bert nodded but called out of the door, 'Who's injured up there?'

Reggie's voice came back, 'Graham Soper skipper. Nasty shrapnel cut to his scalp but I've dressed it as best I can.'

'Good lad Reggie. If he can walk, get him aft to the cook. He's had more experience with wounds. Don't leave him if Dougie's not there though.'

'Will do skipper!'

Bert spun back as a thought hit him, 'Oh, Reggie. When Soper is with Dougie, can you check the depth charges, seeing as shrapnel has been flying?'

'No problem skipper,' came the faint reply.

Nobby came out of his wireless room, 'Order from Dover skipper, look for survivors. I've acknowledged.'

'Thanks Nobby. Helm, take us toward that fire.' Bert glanced at Mather who nodded toward the wireless room. Bert turned, 'Nobby we need your room for two minutes, please?'

'Nae bother skipper, I'll fetch us a brew.'

As the door closed behind them Mather cleared his throat, 'Skipper, the lads at the gun hadn't seen the mate when I got there. He seems to have been elsewhere during the action. I'd have thought nothing of it until he said he'd go back to the gun which I had just left...'

Bert nodded slowly, 'I think this needs exploring Mr Mather. He may finally have slipped up. I'll talk to him directly. Would you check Reggie has got Soper sorted out please? I sent him aft to get the cook to have a look.'

Mr Mather nodded, and they left the radio room.

Bert looked down and saw Cummings leaning over the rail, smoking. Against his orders but, given the view ahead looked like bonfire night, not really an issue. He slowly walked down the steps, coming up behind Cummings.

'Why didn't you go to the gun when I ordered you to do so? I'm asking about the first time, during the firing, and now.'

There was a flurry of sparks as the cigarette hit the toe rail and spiralled down to the black water.

'I, well, I thought I heard something hit the deckhouse, so I went to check skipper.'

Bert took a deep breath, 'It took you ten minutes to check for damage?'

Cummings' voice became harder, 'I thought I smelled electrical burning. Any issues with that?'

Bert paused, 'If I believed you, then no, I'd have no issues at all. As things stand I believe you have questions to answer. We have been tasked to find survivors so you will go to the gun, then assist as necessary depending upon what we find. In the fullness of time we will discuss your conduct and what follows from that. Oh, and if I see you smoking at night again I will put you in irons. Now MOVE!'

Cummings huffed away forward and Bert caught a muttered, 'they're all in it together.' Sighing, he went quickly back to the wheelhouse

As they approached, a British destroyer signalled them to assist the search and after forty minutes they had found one British and one German survivor.

Mather looked at the two young lads, thinking that, with blankets wrapped around them, it was impossible to tell nationalities apart. The desperate sadness of war was overpowering, but he was wise enough to know that the voices of patriotism and crowd mentality were yet more powerful. He shook his head and went to loook for Reggie.

Ten minutes later, a British destroyer torpedoed the burning ship and darkness returned. A tug had arrived to tow a damaged British destroyer back to Dover and another German ship was sunk by gunfire after her crew had been taken off by other tugs.

Reggie was giving hot tea to the survivors. He learned the German lad was called Joachim and tried to reassure him in the few words of German he had. The English lad, was in shock but physically alright. He had apparently been flung overboard when his ship rammed a German destroyer.

They were stood down from action stations and half the crew sent to eat while the others squared away after the action.

Cummings grumbled about 'fraternising with the enemy' but seemed otherwise subdued so Reggie just carried on with his duties. After half an hour however, Cummings had worked himself up into a filthy temper. He sent Reggie below to help the Engineer, saying he could eat when he had finished. Henry, the engineer, was an affable old fellow from Grimsby and asked Reggie to sort a spares cupboard which had spilled some of its contents when they had turned. He said he was popping off to get a brew and Reggie should eat when he had done, 'So far as the mate is concerned I've been slave driving you all the time you were down here.' He gave a broad wink and set off up the ladder. Reggie had just locked the cupboard and gone to wipe his hands with some cotton waste which he knew was kept nearer the boiler, when he heard Cummings' voice.

'Where are you, you little bastard?' he yelled.

Reggie knew Colin was in the wheelhouse and blew into the speaking tube, then covered it with his hand as a voice answered. He flipped the cover right back and hissed 'Just listen Colin!' before standing in front of the tube. Cummings stormed toward him.

'I've had a belly full of you and your gang Hurton. What's the story? Daddy had a word with the skipper to put a knife into me?'

'Chief, I don't know what you're talking about. My father apprenticed me into this ship because he knew the skipper is good at training his lads. He did that because he wanted the exact opposite of what you keep saying, he didn't want to risk showing favouritism toward me by keeping me on his own ship.' Reggie held his ground, hoping Colin was listening. He went on, 'I just don't understand where all this comes from, are you...'

'HOW DARE YOU!,' Cummings screamed incoherently, 'Your name is enough Hurton. You have no idea what your father did to me, what I had to live with after he cut me out!'

Reggie shook his head, 'But Chief, it was you who did the damage, you had lied in your application and told him you were more experienced than you were. He turned you down after finding that out. Now you really are the mate of a ship so you've been successful in the end, surely?'

Cummings seemed to deflate a little, but picked up a Stilson wrench, 'So you're spouting the company line now are you? No harm done? I swore I'd pay your father back, and it felt like fate when you fell into my hands. I was showing you for what you really are, but had no hint the skipper was part of your cosy little gang. He's trying to stab me in the back, it seems, so this is my only chance.

Reggie screwed up his eyes, 'And how, pray tell, are you going to do that?'

Cummings missed Reggie's attempt to goad him and grinned, hefting the wrench, 'Well, you're about to bump your head and fall overboard. Such a sad loss.'

Reggie knew he'd pushed his luck as far as he could so he twisted away from the mate, skipped across the gantry and ran for the step-over which bridged the shaft. Cummings initially began to follow but realised Reggie's intent and turned to run. He knew Reggie had the legs on him so dropped the wrench and sprinted. Reggie was just four or five steps above his swinging arm as he reached the ladder. They both climbed frantically.

At the top, Reggie ran straight down the short passage and out onto the afterdeck. He realised he couldn't hide behind the equipment locker, so turned where he had space to move, fervently hoping Colin had heard what happened. Cummings advanced, fists clenched. He had no words now, just a feral snarl and black hatred on his face.

Reggie ducked his first swing and slammed his fist into Cummings' ribs. Cummings brought his elbow back and rammed it into Reggie's temple. Reggie saw tiny lights for a split second, but Cummings was pulling his fist back, leaving his midriff open. Reggie hooked his right hand up, aiming for the solar plexus. It was a good contact but didn't wind Cummings as much as he hoped. Cummings spun him and threw a punch which rammed his eye socket. Reggie tripped backward and lifted his head to see Cummings pull a wicked-looking clasp knife from his pocket. Cummings snarled, madness in his eyes.

'Now to do some gutting, you little runt.'

Reggie swung a huge kick which sent the knife skittering across the deck. Cummings bared his teeth and dragged Reggie up by his lapels, 'Alright, just the swim then.' Reggie kept calm and pretended to flop his head back, then slammed his head forward in a head-butt which laid Cummings on his back.

Reggie was stunned by the force of his blow and bent, hands on knees, shaking his head. Cummings had spittle at the edges of his mouth and blood running from his nostrils as he clawed for his knife with his right hand. He felt the knurled handle and grasped it, his eyes bulging. He started forward just as Mr Mather's boot stamped down, crushing his fingers.

'Cummings, I heard what you said to Mr Hurton and The Skipper and others were listening in the wheelhouse to what was said in the engineroom. You will face charges as a result.'

Back in Dover, Cummings stood in the aft cabin, head bowed. The skipper sat behind the table at the stern. Reggie, Mr Mather, Colin, McNab and Phillips, all of whom had given evidence, stood to the side.

The skipper spoke, 'Chief Petty Officer Cummings, I have heard the evidence and I find you have a case to answer which requires more authority than I possess. I am therefore referring you ashore for court marshal.'

Cummings looked up, 'Good, I'll be able to say how you mismanage this ship and are more loyal to your little gang of mates than to the Royal Navy. I think you'll fi...'

'Take him away Mr Smith. As of now you are acting first mate. You can use the aft heads as a brig. He'll only be there for a few hours,' he looked up, 'Shut up Cummings.'

Chapter 8

The Healing

His Majesty's Trawler Auriga slipped her cable and left Dover Harbour. On the mess-deck, Reggie stood with McNab in front of Bilton, Soper and Challener.

Reggie coughed, 'I wanted a word lads, before we get busy. What happened can't be changed but I want you to know I realise Cummings was damned clever and could manipulate anyone. There are no hard feelings here, alright?'

The three nodded, but looked surly. Reggie was happy. The atmosphere wouldn't clear instantly, but it was a start.

Later that day they were swinging out the boat to repair a buoy light on the barrage. His three former tormentors were heading to the falls and Reggie hopped up the ladder.

'Can I give you a hand lads?'

Challener looked hard at him, then grinned, 'Aye lad, we could use you. You're alright by us.'

Reggie smiled back, 'Good news. Right then, let's get after it!'

Chapter 9

The Parting

In June, Bert, Colin and Reggie stood facing Mr Mather as he shook their hands, 'I wish you all the luck in the world, gentlemen. Thank you for your help and understanding; I'm not an ordinary naval officer: as you know I'm just a scientist who was given a uniform, so thanks for putting up with my foibles.'

Bert grinned, 'Well Mr Mather, we're actually fishermen who were given uniforms so we aren't so different I'd say.'

Mather laughed, 'We're not at that skipper. Right, I'm off. If they run any more trials, I shall ask for your ship if you don't mind. Oh, and, Reggie, remember what I said: you helped to improve our hydrophone design, so every time you hear a sub was sunk, you should be proud.'

They waved him off before hopping over the bulwark to the ship.

Chapter 10

Epilogue

NOVEMBER 1918

Bert slapped his hands together for warmth as he returned to the ship. He was dropped off by a harbour launch as it passed HMT Auriga. The greyness of dawn gave way to the greyness of a wet early November day. He called for a brew and looked around the wheelhouse. So many memories, mostly bad; but the good ones were very good. He laughed at himself as he sipped on his sweet tea.

An hour later Colin and Reggie came in. Colin glanced over, 'Now then skipper, what's the news ashore?'

Bert nodded, looking sombre, 'Well, they're saying it'll be over soon. Perhaps within days. That's hopeful news. There was something else.'

Reggie turned to face Bert, 'Are you alright skipper?'

Bert nodded, 'I am, lad. It's strange news, really. As you know the van driver taking Cummings to the jail stopped for a pie and he did a runner. Cummings flat disappeared, but I learned he was arrested by the civilian police. He had attacked and killed the young woman who had sheltered him for all that time. He'd met her while in the Navy so nobody who knew him before the war was aware of her. Anyway, there was a trial and guilty verdict. The Navy wanted him shot as a deserter but civil law prevailed and he was hung last week.'

Reggie blew out his cheeks, 'Sad. He was an evil bugger but I often wonder what happened in his past to damage him that much.'

Bert nodded, 'Well he made his own bed, that's certain. I must be straight, I'm glad in one respect. As long as he was out there I feared he'd attack you, Reggie, or your father. Anyway, it's done now. No knife in the back for you.'

There was silence for a moment before Colin spoke, 'I don't know about that skipper. Have you heard him snoring?'

On the harbour launch, the shivering naval rating, who was getting his boathook ready, looked up at a sudden noise, 'Strewth. Only a ruddy fisherman would find this weather funny!'

THE END

Afterword

I hope you liked this short introduction to The Skipper Series.

If you have time, I'd love you to review this novella on Amazon, you can also leave feedback, comments or requests on my blog, (https://mark-tissington-author.blogspot.com). If you prefer direct messaging, please use the Wandering Tree Publications website form (https://www.wtpublicat ions.com/contact)

If you haven't already subscribed to my newsletter, please got to https://subscribepage.io/zMC2Ri

MARK TISSINGTON

WANDERING TREE PUBLICATIONS LIMITED

Printed in Great Britain
by Amazon

26490836R00046